The First Christmas

by Robbie Trent

pictures by Marc Simont

Harper & Row, Publishers

The First Christmas

Typography by Patricia Tobin
1 2 3 4 5 6 7 8 9 10
New Edition

Library of Congress Cataloging-in-Publication Data
Trent, Robbie.
The first Christmas / by Robbie Trent ; pictures by Marc Simont. —New ed.
p. cm.
Summary: A simple retelling of how Jesus Christ came to be born in a stable.
ISBN 0-06-026165-X : $. ISBN 0-06-026166-8 (lib. bdg.) $. ISBN 0-06-443249-1 (Harper trophy book : pbk.) : $.
1. Jesus Christ—Nativity—Juvenile literature. [1. Jesus Christ—Nativity.] I. Simont, Marc, ill. II. Title.
BT315.T7 1990 89-29729
232.92'1—dc20 CIP
AC

The First Christmas

This is Mary.

This is the donkey
that Mary rode
to Bethlehem.

This is Joseph
who led the donkey
that Mary rode.

This is the town
of Bethlehem
where Mary and Joseph
were going.

This is the inn
where Mary and Joseph
could find no room.

This is the stable
where Mary and Joseph
rested in Bethlehem.

These are the shepherds
out in the fields
near Bethlehem.

These are the dogs
that were helping
the shepherds to keep
the sheep safe.

This is the moon
that the shepherds saw
in the nighttime sky.

This is the angel
bringing glad news,
"Little Jesus is born
in Bethlehem."

This is the road
where the shepherds
went running to find
the baby in Bethlehem.

This is the manger
filled with hay
that the shepherds saw
in the stable.

"Away in the manger,
No crib for a bed,
The little Lord Jesus
Laid down His sweet head;
The stars in the sky
Looked down where He lay,
The little Lord Jesus
Asleep on the hay."

Old Hymn